To **Alexander**

For being good.
MERRY CHRISTMAS!

From Maisie -Rose,
Tilly & Barclay

It was a crisp Christmas Eve
and Santa and his reindeers
were busy delivering presents to
all the good boys and girls.

Santa's sleigh zoomed over houses, twisting
and turning silently through the snowy night sky.
Santa squeezed down and up and up and down
chimneys, carefully and quietly delivering
lots of presents.

4

...was going to
...lan until he
...eached the
...cond to last
...se on his list.

Suddenly,
Santa noticed one of
the presents was **missing!**

The reindeer looked in Santa's sack,
they searched **everywhere** but the
present was nowhere to be found!
"Oh no!" exclaimed Santa. "It must
have fallen off
the sleigh!"

Santa wondered what to do.
He had no time to look for the present
but he didn't want to disappoint anyone
on his Christmas list.

Then
Santa had a
FANTASTIC
idea!

He looked at his delivery map to see where they were.
Then he checked his list to see who had been naughty or n

At the very
top of the list was Alexander.
So Santa and Blitzen (the smallest of
all the reindeer) squeezed
down the chimney...

7

his

into

quietly

crept

...and

bedroom.

Alexander yawned,
stretched and rubbed
his eyes. He thought he
was still **dreaming** until Blitzen licked his
face with his long, wet, pink tongue - YUCK!

8

"I need your help!" boomed Santa. He explained that a present had fallen off the sleigh and Santa wanted **Alexander** to go with Blitzen to find it.

Alexander of course was VERY happy to help.

It was cold and snowy outside so Alexander put on his warmest hat and long, stripy scarf.

Alexander and Blitzen looked through Santa's telescope.

They looked down past the houses and through the trees, trying to find the lost present.

Suddenly they spotted it, sitting on top of a pile of snow at the bottom of a big hill.

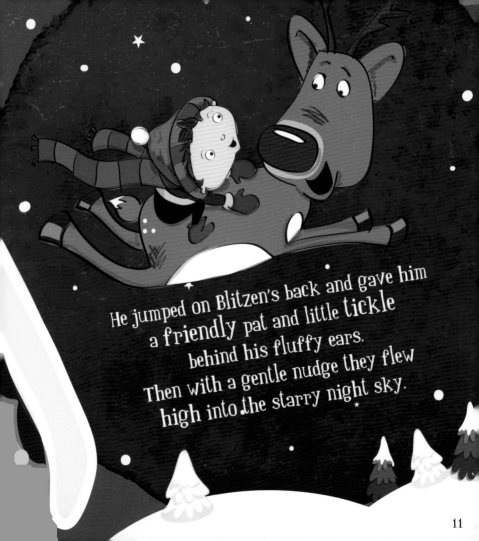

He jumped on Blitzen's back and gave him
a friendly pat and little tickle
behind his fluffy ears.
Then with a gentle nudge they flew
high into the starry night sky.

11

Up and up they soared

and higher
higher

until Blitzen did a
loop the loop,
a flip and a flop
and landed with a bop
next to the pile of snow...

but the present had gone

12

lexander and Blitzen looked around but couldn't see the present anywhere!

ll of a sudden Blitzen's wet nose began to itch and itch and wibble and wobble. What had he found?

xander saw a bright orange carrot sticking out of the snow. "Who likes carrots?" he wondered. Perhaps this was a clue to where the present had gone.

Then they saw a tiny white and grey bunny rab[bit].

"Hello Mrs Rabbit, we're **looking** for a missing gift which fell from Santa's sleigh. Have you seen **anything**[?]"

The bunny **twitched** her nose, rubbed her ears and **pointed** a fluffy white paw at a line of acorns.

"Who likes acorns?"
wondered Alexander.

Then looking down, they noticed a
bouncy red squirrel staring back at them.
They followed him, picking up the acorns one by one,
knowing who or what would be at the end of the trail.

As they picked up the final acorn, they noticed a nose-less, button-less, very sad snowman right in front of them.

His carrot nose had fallen off and his acorn buttons had been lost but there, poking out fro under his black ha was a shiny Christmas present

16

Hurray, they had found the present...
but why did the snowman have it?

The sad snowman explained that
every year he felt forgotten as
he never received a present.
When he found this one he was so
happy. However, now he knew
it belonged to someone
else, he wanted to
give it back.

17

Feeling sorry for the snowman, **Alexander** decided to help.
He placed the half-eaten carrot on the snowman's face for his nose and the acorn buttons on his body but the snowman still looked sad.

Then **Alexander** had a brilliant idea!

He undid his fluffy scarf and tied it around the surprised snowman.

Then he replaced the snowman's old black hat with his warm knitted one.

The snowman was so happy! At last he had his very OWN Christmas present!

Alexander and Blitzen flew as fast as they could to get the missing present back in time for Christmas morning.

Back at home Alexander gave Blitzen a big hug, then watched as his new friend flew up into the sky and home to Santa.

Alexander placed the gift under the tree with a huge sigh of relief!

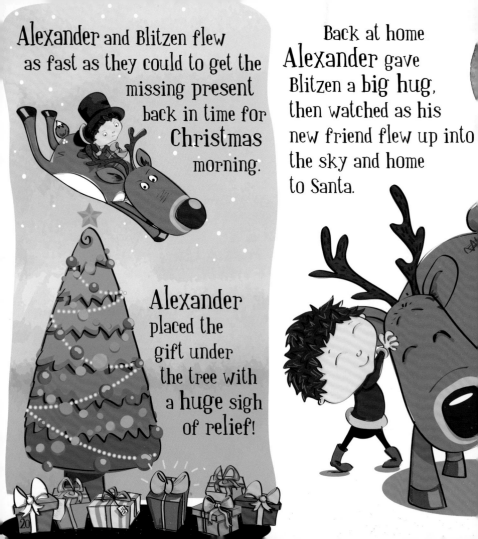

When Alexander woke up on Christmas morning, he wondered if it had all been a dream. Then he looked out of his window...

...and there in the distance was the **happy** snowman waving at him and he was still wearing his **lovely** Christmas present.

The end

21